Puppy Takes a Bath

by Christine Ricci
illustrated by Tom Mangano

Ready-to-Read

Simon Spotlight/Nick Jr.
New York   London   Toronto   Sydney

Based on the TV series *Dora the Explorer*® as seen on Nick Jr.®

SIMON SPOTLIGHT
An imprint of Simon & Schuster Children's Publishing Division
1230 Avenue of the Americas, New York, New York 10020
© 2006 Viacom International Inc. All rights reserved. NICK JR., *Dora the Explorer*, and all
related titles, logos, and characters are registered trademarks of
Viacom International Inc.

Manufactured in the United States of America
16 18 20 19 17
Library of Congress Cataloging-in-Publication Data
Ricci, Christine.
Puppy takes a bath / by Christine Ricci ; illustrated by Tom Mangano.— 1st ed.
p. cm.— (Ready-to-read)
"Dora the explorer."
"Based on the TV series Dora the explorer, as seen on Nick Jr."
ISBN-13: 978-1-4169-1483-9
ISBN-10: 1-4169-1483-8
0811 LAK
I. Mangano, Tom. II. Dora the explorer (Television program) III. Title. IV. Series.
PZ7.R355Pu 2006
2005031340

Hi! I am Dora.

This is my puppy.

My puppy loves
to roll in the dirt.

My puppy needs a bath!

Here is a tub of water.

Backpack has the soap
and the towel.

Help me find them!

The bath is ready.

But where is my puppy'

Is my puppy

hiding in the bushes?

No! My puppy is not
in the bushes.

Is my puppy hiding

in the flowers?

No! My puppy is not
in the flowers.

Is my puppy hiding

in the doghouse?

No! My puppy is not
in the doghouse.

I have an idea!

Here is a bone.

Here is my puppy!

My puppy sees the bone.

My puppy likes his bath.

My puppy is all clean!